Winnie's
Awful Auntie

LAURA OWEN & KORKY PAUL

OXFORD
UNIVERSITY PRESS

Helping your child to read

Before they start

⭑ Talk about the back cover blurb. What sort of person does Winnie's Auntie Aggie sound like? What does your child think will happen when she comes to stay with Winnie?

⭑ Look at the picture on the front cover. Does it give your child any clues about what might happen in the stories?

During reading

⭑ Let your child read at their own pace – don't worry if it's slow. They could read silently, or read to you out loud.

⭑ Help them to work out words they don't know by saying each sound out loud and then blending them to say the word, e.g. *a-ll-i-g-a-t-o-r*, *alligator*.

⭑ If your child still struggles with a word, just tell them the word and move on.

⭑ Give them lots of praise for good reading!

After reading

⭑ Look at page 48 for some fun activities.

Contents

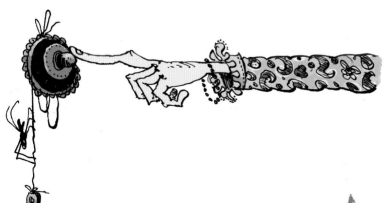

OXFORD
UNIVERSITY PRESS

Great Clarendon Street, Oxford OX2 6DP
Oxford University Press is a department of the University of Oxford.
It furthers the University's objective of excellence in research, scholarship,
and education by publishing worldwide. Oxford is a registered trade mark
of Oxford University Press in the UK and in certain other countries

Text © Oxford University Press
Illustrations © Korky Paul

The characters in this work are the original creation of Valerie Thomas
who retains copyright in the characters.

"Winnie the Naughty Niece" was first published in *Winnie Spells Trouble* in 2014
"Winnie's Auntie Trouble" was first published as "Winnie's Awful Auntie" in *Mini Winnie* in 2008
This edition published 2019

The moral rights of the author/illustrator have been asserted

Database right Oxford University Press (maker)

British Library Cataloguing in Publication Data

Data available

ISBN: 978-0-19-276917-6

3 5 7 9 10 8 6 4 2

OX27868901

Printed in China

Paper used in the production of this book is a natural,
recyclable product made from wood grown in sustainable forests.
The manufacturing process conforms to the environmental
regulations of the country of origin.

Acknowledgements
With thanks to Catherine Baker for editorial support

Winnie the Naughty Niece

6

✫ Chapter ✫ One

Winnie was looking in the fridge. "What shall we have for lunch, Wilbur?" she asked.

"Purr!" said Wilbur.

"That's a brilliant idea!" said Winnie. "Flied eggs on toast!"

There were two eggs left: a snake egg and an alligator egg.

"Now we need some yummy fresh flies to go with the eggs!" said Winnie.

7

Winnie and Wilbur went out into the garden. Lots of flies were buzzing around the compost heap. Winnie smelled the pong of rotting grass.

Brrrrm! Jerry, the giant next door, was mowing his lawn. That was where the grass cuttings came from.

"Hide, Wilbur!" hissed Winnie. "If Jerry sees us, we'll have to invite him for lunch, but we've only got two eggs!"

So they hid behind the compost heap.
They tried to catch flies, but the flies were
too fast.

"Flapping flip-flops!" said Winnie.
"Oooh, I know a sort of lizard that's good
at catching flies. It's called a chameleon."
She waved her wand. "**Abracadabra!**"

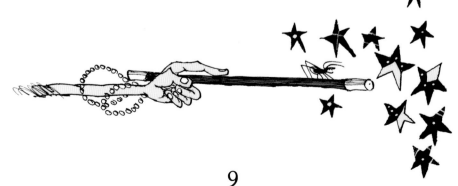

Suddenly, there was a chameleon.

Flick-slurp! The chameleon picked up
a fly with its sticky tongue. Winnie and
Wilbur both jumped. They hadn't seen
the green chameleon sitting on a branch!
The chameleon snatched another fly and
ate it.

"Hey!" said Winnie. "You're supposed to
be giving the flies to us!"

The chameleon spat the next fly into
Winnie's hand. It went on catching more
and more. Every time it made Winnie jump.

Soon, the chameleon had caught lots of
flies. But then it vanished!

"Where's that little chameleon gone
now?" said Winnie.

Flick-slurp!

At last Winnie saw the chameleon. He was purple, and sitting on her cardigan.

Flick-slurp!

Now he'd gone blue on Winnie's shoe.

"We've got enough flies now," said Winnie. "Let's go back to the house and start cooking!"

But just then they heard someone shouting at Winnie's front door.

"Winifred Witch, open the door! Your Auntie Aggie is here!"

Gulp! went Winnie. "Oh no! Auntie Aggie can't stay for lunch because we've only got two eggs! She'll go away if we hide."

✫ Chapter ✫ Two

Auntie Aggie waved her pink plastic wand. "**Abracadabra!**" Winnie's front door opened wide, and Auntie Aggie marched into the house.

"What a cheek!" said Winnie. "Now what can we do?"

Flick-slurp! Jump! The chameleon jumped on to Wilbur's fur. It turned black, so Winnie could hardly see it.

"Brilliant!" said Winnie. "That chameleon has given me a plan. I know how we can get into the house and cook our flied eggs without Auntie Aggie seeing us."

She waved her wand. "**Abracadabra!**"

Suddenly, both Winnie and Wilbur were covered in sticky treacle.

"Meeow?" asked Wilbur.

"Don't lick it off, Wilbur. It's glue, not food." Winnie jumped on to the compost heap, and rolled about. Soon she was covered in leaves. Wilbur copied her. They looked like bushes – a witchy one and a catty one.

"Now, creep up the path to the door. Auntie Aggie will never guess it's us!" said Winnie.

Winnie and Wilbur really did look like bushes. When Scruff from next door saw them, he lifted a leg and . . .

"Meeow!" hissed the Wilbur bush.

When Winnie and Wilbur got inside, they had a problem.

"Er, what will Auntie Aggie think if she sees bushes indoors?" said Winnie. So she waved a twig, and whispered, "**Abracadabra!**"

Now Winnie looked like a tall lampstand, and Wilbur looked like a furry footstool.

They froze when they heard Auntie
Aggie coming into the hall.

"What a silly place to leave an ugly
great lamp!" said Auntie Aggie.

"Come on, Wilbur!" hissed Winnie the
lampstand. Winnie and Wilbur started to
shuffle towards the kitchen. But just then,
Auntie Aggie turned round. They stopped still.

✦ Chapter ✦ Three

"It's very dark in this horrible house," said Auntie Aggie. "I shall turn on the light." She pulled Winnie's necklace as if it were the light switch.

"Ow!" said Winnie the lampstand.

No light came on. "How strange!" said Auntie Aggie.

Auntie Aggie looked at Wilbur the footstool. "This scruffy footstool needs a good clean," she said, waving her wand. "**Abracadabra!**"

Suddenly, a vacuum cleaner was sucking Wilbur's fur.

"Meeow!" said Wilbur the footstool. All the dust made Winnie the lampstand sneeze.

"Aha, I knew it!" said Auntie Aggie. "Come out at once, Winifred and Wilbur!"

So Winnie and Wilbur came out. Winnie thought she was going to get told off.

But Auntie Aggie laughed. "What a
fun game," she said. "Much better than
ordinary hide-and-seek. Let's all have lunch,
Winifred, and then we can play again."

"B-b-but we were going to have flied eggs
for lunch," said Winnie. "And we've only got
two eggs!"

"Oh, phooey, what do you think a wand is for?" said Auntie Aggie. She waved her pink plastic wand and said, "**Abracadabra!**"

Suddenly, there was an ostrich egg and a
hummingbird egg and a hen egg and a toad
egg and a crocodile egg.

"The ostrich egg is for your big neighbour,
Jerry," said Auntie Aggie. "I invited him to
lunch. I hope you don't mind."

Winnie didn't mind at all, because now there was enough food for everyone.

After lunch they all played a game of hide-and-shriek. And who do you think won? The chameleon!

Winnie's Auntie Trouble

✯ Chapter ✯ One

Ding-dong! Winn-eeeee! went the doorbell.

Winnie woke up. "What was that noise, Wilbur?"

Wilbur rolled over, stretched, yawned, and went back to sleep.

Winnie lay down again, too. But just as she was about to fall asleep . . .

Brriiing! Winn-eeeee! went the doorbell.

Winnie peeped out of the window. "Oh, bees' boots!" she said. "It's Auntie Aggie. Look at all that luggage! I think she's come to stay with us!"

Wilbur hid under the sheets.

"I'll be down before you can say, 'mouldy maggots', Auntie Aggie," Winnie yelled. She picked up her wand. "I'd better make this house smell right for an aunt. **Abracadabra!**" At once, the lovely mouldy smell vanished. The whole house filled up with a pink rosy-posy pong.

"Meeow!" Wilbur put a paw to his nose.

So Winnie got out two clothes pegs. She stuck one on her nose, and one on Wilbur's nose.

"Winifred Witch, will you please open this door?" yelled Auntie Aggie.

"Look out, Wilbur," said Winnie. "I'm going to let her in."

Auntie Aggie pointed at Winnie's clothes peg, and said, "What in the world is *that* for?"

"Well," said Winnie, "it's the new fashion." But Auntie Aggie wasn't listening.

"How silly you are!" she said. "Take it off at once."

"Yes, Auntie Aggie," said Winnie.

Auntie Aggie pulled a hanky from her sleeve. She spat on it, then she wiped it over Winnie's face.

"Yeuch, get off!" said Winnie.

"I've come to sort you out, young lady," said Auntie Aggie.

"But I don't . . ." began Winnie.

"Don't argue!" said Auntie Aggie. "Now, where to begin?" She looked around the kitchen and tutted. "Dear, oh dear!" She bent over, sticking her large bottom in the air, as she took rubber gloves from her bag, and pulled them on.

Auntie Aggie waved her wand. "Spit spot!" she shouted. All Winnie's stuff zoomed up on to shelves and into cupboards.

Slam-slam went the cupboard doors.

"Now I won't know where anything is!" wailed Winnie.

"Nonsense!" said Auntie Aggie. "I'll smarten you up next."

"But I don't . . ." began Winnie.

"Spit spot!" went Auntie Aggie, and at once Winnie was wearing a smart suit. Her hair was short and neat.

Wilbur was tittering into his paws. "Mee-hee-hee-ow!"

⭐ Chapter ⭐ Two

Next, Auntie Aggie looked at Wilbur.
"I must do something about that
stinky cat!" she said. She lifted her
wand and . . .

"No!" said Winnie. She leaped towards
Wilbur, but her suit skirt was too tight.
Bang! She fell on the floor.

Suddenly, Wilbur wasn't a cat any more.

"What have you done, Auntie Aggie?"
wailed Winnie. "Where's my Wilbur?"

"He's become a sweet little, clean little
rabbit," said Auntie Aggie.

"But I want *Wilbur*!" wailed Winnie.
"My Wilbur! I'm a witch, not a magician!
Change Wilbur back!"

"No way," said Auntie Aggie. "You young people don't know what's best. You'll soon love Wilbur the rabbit more than you ever loved that stinky cat. He can live in a nice pink cage."

"Never!" said Winnie. She gazed deep into the rabbit's eyes. She could see the real Wilbur trapped inside the silly face with floppy ears. Poor Wilbur!

Auntie Aggie looked at Winnie crossly. "You wait, Winifred," she said. "When I'm an old witch I won't be able to help you like this, and then you'll be sorry!"

Suddenly, there was a strange noise in the room. **Twitter-twee, twitter-twee.**

"It's my phone," said Auntie Aggie. "I'll be back in a jiffy."

She dashed into the garden to answer the phone.

"Don't panic, Wilbur!" said Winnie. "I'll rescue you! But first I'm going to magic Auntie Aggie."

"Snuffle?" asked Wilbur.

"Yes," said Winnie. "Remember how Auntie Aggie said she won't be able to do magic on us once she's an old lady?"

"Snuffle," Wilbur said.

"Well, I'm going to turn her into an old lady until she goes back home. Then I'll get you back, Wilbur!"

"Snuffle! Snuffle!" Wilbur said.

As Auntie Aggie came back indoors, Winnie waved her wand. She wished, "Make Auntie Aggie much, much older than me. **Abracadabra!**"

Gasp! went Auntie Aggie.

Gasp-nibble! went Wilbur the rabbit.

"Waaah!" went a little baby on the floor.

Wilbur glared at Winnie's wand but there was nothing wrong with Winnie's magic.

Auntie Aggie *was* much older than
Winnie, because Winnie was a baby now.

Baby Winnie kicked her legs and waved
her fists. Then suddenly baby Winnie went
quiet and a stinky smell filled the room.

Chapter Three

"Eeek!" shrieked Auntie Aggie. "I can't stand babies! Noisy, smelly things! I had to wait ages until you were grown up, Winnie, and now look what in the witchy world you've done!"

"Waaah!" went baby Winnie again.

"Poooooey! Oooh, dear!" said Auntie Aggie. "Quick, where's that clothes peg? That's it, I'm off!" And she grabbed her bags and rushed away down the road.

But Winnie was still a baby. She got on
to her hands and knees and crawled at top
speed out of the door.

Snuffle-nibble! went Wilbur the rabbit.
He picked up Winnie's wand.

Then he hopped all over the lawn waving the wand. **Boing! Boing!** He hopped in the shape of an "a". **Boing! Boing!** Then he hopped in the shape of a "b" and then an "r" . . . until he spelled out the whole of "**Abracadabra!**"

At once, Winnie was back to her old self.

"Well done, Wilbur!" she said. Then she waved the wand. "**Abracadabra!**"

Suddenly, Wilbur was himself again, too.

"Meeow!" said Wilbur. "Meeow, meeow, meeow!"

"Yes," said Winnie. "But I think we've got rid of Auntie Aggie!" Winnie gave Wilbur a big hug. "Oooh, Wilbur, I'm so very, very glad you're not really a rabbit!"

After reading activities

Quick quiz

See how fast you can answer these
questions! Look back at the stories if
you can't remember.

1) In "Winnie the Naughty Niece", what two
   things does Winnie disguise herself as?
2) In "Winnie the Naughty Niece", how does
   Auntie Aggie solve the problem of not having
   enough eggs for everyone?
3) In "Winnie's Auntie Trouble", how does
   Winnie's plan to turn Auntie Aggie into an old
   lady go wrong?

1) a bush and a lampstand; 2) she magics up some more eggs; 3) Winnie ends up turning herself into a baby

Talk about it!

* How do you think Winnie feels about Auntie
  Aggie at the end of "Winnie the Naughty
  Niece"? Does Auntie Aggie still seem like an
  "Awful Auntie"? Why, or why not?
* Why do you think Auntie Aggie wanted to
  smarten everything up in "Winnie's Auntie
  Trouble"? Do you think it was right to do
  this? How did it make Winnie feel?